From Acorns To Angels

[signature: Sam Wallace]

By
Samuel H Wallace

www.xulonpress.com

Chapter One

Reflecting On The Beginning

*A*s I sit here in this old antique store, in the same spot for a year, dust has settled over me. In the distance I can see through the window to a cold and dreary day. The sky is covered with clouds and it has begun to rain.

I guess this is "it" whatever "it" is. My long life is over. I must be destined to spend eternity in this place. Unlike man that goes to sleep and never wakes up when he is old, I continue to wake daily, not knowing if I will ever escape this old lonely building away from everything. An exciting span of nearly 250 years has seemed to come to a sudden stop.

My past was one of learning, the knowledge and patience that I have learned simply by watching and listening could fill an entire book. I have learned of life and death, of love and hate. I am not a scholar or even a person of great wisdom. In fact, I am not a person at all. I am just an old bed. However, I was not always a bed. I was a tree at one time. A great, mighty oak tree. You may ask, what knowledge can a tree gain from being in one spot so long. Well, if you are in the right spot and stand there long enough, watch and listen, you can open up to whole world that you never knew existed.

As far back as I remember, it all started in the spring of 1756, before I was a tree, I was just an acorn hanging from my mother tree, and boy did I have a view.

In the distance I could see snowcaps on the Great Smoky Mountains. I could see other bloom filled trees for miles. I could also see a stream that was surrounded by life, from the plants and animals beside it, to the fish that were jumping in the current. My life was just as good as my view. I started as all young oaks do, as an acorn. All spring and summer I had no worry. I thought my whole life would be spent just hanging there. Then, come fall, I began seeing other acorns fall one by one. Then I knew that I too, would fall.

How was I going to make it when I had to survive on my own? I soon found the answer to my tormenting question. It came one evening, late in the fall, as a strong wind blew. I knew that my time had come. I realized that I must not fall to the ground, instead I would glide, for I have only one chance to go down gracefully, I can... Suddenly, I lost everything, every thought that I had about going down gracefully was gone. At that instant a strong wind blew, and the last few fibers that held my stem to my mother tree were ripped free and I spiraled down. Reality set in and I knew I had control of nothing and I just hoped that none of my brothers and sisters saw my descent. When the leaves fell, they would glide down in such grace until they would come to rest upon the ground. But me, I fell straight down and hit the ground with a great big thump. Then, I began to roll. I rolled down the hill passed the other trees until I finally stopped. As I looked around I could no longer see my mother tree. The world as I knew it was changed forever. For just one minute ago I was on the top of the world looking down, and now everything that I looked down upon was above me. I then realized that the impression that I had made on them with my descent did not matter anymore.

As it was getting dark I could feel the cold wind blow across my shell. I then realized that I was on my own. I could not get up to walk. I could not build a fire to warm me. All I knew was to just lay there, look and listen.

Just as soon as the night came, it was gone. In the morning I could see the light of the sun. As the day passed, there were different times when the sunlight would pass through the trees that were around me and would warm my shell. I soon learned that things that I had taken for granted, such as hanging in the sun all day should have been appreciated. For now, each time I felt it, it was precious to me. Now as the nights get colder, it is something that I look forward to each day.

One morning I was waiting for my little glimpse of sun after a cold night, there were leaves that began to fall all around me. They began to block my view of most of my surroundings. As I sat, waiting for my glimpse of the sun, I could hear footsteps on the leaves. As the crunching of the leaves got closer, I could see, for the first time, a small baby deer and his mother. I remember how they would play and rub against each other and it gave me a longing to be back with my mother, but that would not happen. I soon slipped back into reality and was filled with fear. Not only were they playing, but the mother deer was eating other acorns that had fallen around me. I could not run or hide, I just hoped that she would not see me. As she ate, she finally wondered off into the distance. I was once again alone, but I was not eaten.

As the leaves began to fall at a faster pace, I began to see the faint outline of my mother in the distance. I could see the branches where acorns and leaves used to hang, that was now picked bare by the gentle hand of fall. I realized that she had worked hard all year long producing her acorns and now her time of rest had come for winter was on its way.

As night falls, my view that was once blocked by leaves changed and for the first time in my short life of five or six months, I can see a full sky that is filled with stars and a moon. Some of the stars are lined up and leave beautiful designs in the sky as if they were painted onto a canvas. Others just sit and sparkle like a diamond in the sun.

I am realizing more as time goes by that although I may have had a bad start, I am lucky. For when I was hanging above everything, all I could do was look down, and now that I am down, I have a chance to look up. And see more beauty than ever before. And this builds a desire within me to rise higher to get closer to the beauty above.

Chapter Two

Fear And Misfortune
Creates A New Life

*A*s winter comes and the snow falls, I am covered with snow for days at a time. I can see nothing but white. Although I am cold and lonely, I am warmed by pleasant memories of my past. The gentle branch on which my mother held me; the flowers and beautiful stars that I had seen; thinking on these things kept me until the snow was gone and once again, I was free.

Once again I heard the sound of footsteps. This time they were smaller and seemed to move a lot faster. As I opened my eyes there I was face to face with a brown squirrel. Before I even had a chance to think, I was in his mouth and gone. His teeth were tight against my shell and we were moving fast. I wondered what would become of me, and just as quick as I was picked up, I was dropped into a hole and the last thing I remember seeing was the squirrel as he covered me up with dirt. I was in shock. Fear had gripped me and I did not know what was going on. I have seen squirrels eat acorns, and I have seen them bury them and eat them later. As I lay in this hole covered with dirt, I am in total darkness. It seems that now not even the most pleasant memories of my past can comfort me, for I could be dug up and eaten at any time. All I could do now was wait and worry. Days turned into weeks and weeks into months, worry was such a part of me, that I began to wish that I would be dug up and eaten, then my troubles would be over and at least I would no longer be troubled with what might happen, but that was not what happened at all. As I spent all that time in darkness, I did not realize that the moist soil above me was growing warmer every day, until one day I began to feel a pressure inside of me. My shell had become soft and it started to break. I could not see what was going on, for I was still in darkness. Every day I began to feel differently. I felt as if I was truly coming to life. I felt movement, it was such a little each day, but it was still movement and that gave me hope.

Then one morning I awoke not only to the warmth that I had felt, but I was able to see a little light through the soil and debris that was still over me. It gave me more hope than I had ever had! For I saw light, and after months in darkness, a little light is still light and that is what I have been longing for, and now that it what I have. As each day passed, each morning would bring more light.

Finally, winter gave way to spring and spring gave way to longer days. One morning, I awoke and was completely out of the soil. I realized that my shell that was once hard and covered me was just as an empty cocoon, and I was no longer an acorn but a small sapling, a baby tree. All of the fear and confusion was over, no longer will I be squirrel food, but now I have a chance at a different life. For now I am oak tree. I am only inches tall, but as I look up I can see other trees that stand 60 to 70 feet tall. They, too, are waking up from their winter rest, with flowers blooming and new leaves growing. I can see tall evergreens of 80 to 90 feet tall start to relax after standing watch all winter. I know that I am just a few inches tall, but I know that this is just the beginning of a journey. A journey that will last an entire lifetime. Not only will I get tall, but I will also get smart, if I can just listen and watch.

Chapter Three

The Joy Of Songs,
The Pains Of Death

I am very thankful for who I am. I am not a person or great machine, but I am me. From my short life of nearly one year, I realize that I could have been less fortunate. Deer or squirrel food would have been misfortune, but I was delivered for some unknown reason. It may have been luck, or it may have been for a purpose. Whatever the reason, I do not know at this time. I will accept what comes, and I will watch and learn from the actions of my surroundings. If I cannot move or accomplish tasks, I will at least have knowledge. For people have crossed oceans, traveled and even died trying to gain knowledge. These people never realize how much they can learn if they just simply stand still and listen.

As I stand here and time goes by, with patience, I watch and listen, the beauty that I remember becomes more visible with every inch that I grow. The sound of birds singing is the music created for the song the trees sing when the wind rustles their leaves. Many people only see and hear what they want to, but if they would truly listen, they could hear things that they have never heard before.

So, did you think a tree just stands there? Not only can we sing, but we dance with the wind as we sing. The songs are for happiness and to comfort each other. For the forest is our family, and we stand together. Some are maples and some are pines; we each have a purpose and we respect one another for who we are. Besides, if you can't get up and leave it is best if everyone just gets long.

As years pass and I grow older, I begin to think that all my lessons have been learned. I have been standing in this same spot for ten years. Everything is the same, my surroundings do not change. Only night and day, winter, spring, summer, and fall, but that is expected.

Early one fall morning, as I stood warming my leaves, I saw that they were turning a beautiful golden color. I knew that fall had come, for the cool mornings let me know that I would soon be at rest for the winter. For I had been growing strong all summer and I had put on more leaves than ever and nearly grew a foot and a half. My roots grew deeper and I was looking forward to the rest that winter would bring. In the distance I could see a deer feeding on acorns. This did not bother me as it had in the past. For I had come to realize that we must all gain nutrition whether it is from the ground as I do or from grass and acorns as the deer. If it does not eat, it will die.

As I stood watching the deer, I did not pay attention to anything else. All I heard was a quick swish and then thump. The deer fell to the ground and just as quickly, it rose, and started to run. He was heading toward me, but he would not run far before he would fall and try to get up again. He made his way within ten feet of me and fell for the last time. I could see an arrow sticking out of his side, and there was blood coming out around it. I did not know what was going on, but I felt scared and helpless. Then, for the first time in my life, I saw man. It was an Indian hunter. He was dressed in deerskin, and had feathers hanging on one side of his head, and a quiver of arrows on his back, and he held his bow in his hands.

As he approached the dying deer, he slowly took a stone knife from his belt and put another hole in the deer's neck. Each time his heart would beat, the blood would run out on the ground. Each time it got slower and less blood flowed until it stopped. The deer was dead.

Every fear and anxiety that I have ever felt came rushing back at that moment. I could not run, I could not cry, and I could not hide, so I just stood there. I have seen old trees die before, but they would just lose their leaves in the fall and not wake up in the spring. Oh, but the death of a living, moving creature as it would struggle to escape or even to survive was more than I have ever thought sad could be.

The hunter walked up to me. He removed the arrows from his back and leaned them against my trunk. Then he put his hand upon me. His fingers, still wet with the blood of the deer, stained my bark. As he leaned against me, I could feel the rapid pulse in his hand. I could feel the warmth, but I could also feel the sadness mixed with joy and I could not understand what was happening until he bowed his head and thanked the Great Spirit for a bountiful hunt. He was grateful that he could feed his family, but he was sad that the deer had to die.

I watched as he cut down two younger trees, and laid them down on each side of the deer. I watched as he put his bow and arrows on the deer and tied them all together. He placed the trees on each of his shoulders and dragged them all away. I watched him until he had disappeared into the distance and I was glad that he was gone. If I would have seen him under different circumstances, it would have been a wonderful experience, but if I never see him again, it will be okay.

I learned so much that day, I felt so many different emotions. I found out what a man was and that they, too, must eat to survive. I found that sometimes, something must die for others to survive. I also found that for some reason, whether it be right or wrong, man makes that call. I just stood there. I watched and listened, for I could not move. The days grew shorter, and the nights got colder. Winter was at hand and my rest had finally come. I may not be over my experience, but at least I will not think of it while I sleep through winter.

Chapter Four

Fire And Strange Music

$\mathcal{T}$ime has been passing so slowly. I have been standing in this spot for over fifty years now. I have experienced many different things in that time. I doubt that anything would surprise me. For I have seen many animals produce and bear their young. I have also seen them care for them and then part ways. I have held the nests of many birds, from sparrows to eagles. I have watched as their young hatched from the eggs that have been so diligently cared for.

And now, for the second time in fifty years I have seen man. And this time I watched as he created fire, and I could smell the smoke that rose from it.

It was in the spring, as I was looking around at all of the new life that was growing around me. I began to hear a sound that I had never heard before. As I listened, it kept getting closer and closer, until I saw movement in the distance. I could see that it was two men. Each man led a pack mule, and on their backs were hundreds of the skins from the animals that they had trapped during the winter. The noise that I had heard was from two cooking pans, tied closely together, on one side of the mule. Each time the animal would take a step, the pans would move, creating the clanging noise. For even this aggravating noise would be a comfort in the middle of nowhere. As they walked towards me, I remembered my last encounter with man, and was ready for anything to happen.

As they walked up to me, out of all of the trees that were around, one of them stopped and tied the rope from his mule to one of my lower branches, and the other to a small sapling nearby. Without a word, they began to unload their mules. They piled the skins into two separate piles, and small bags with food and other supplies in another pile. When the mules had been unpacked, they were led to a small steam were they began to drink. One of the men finally spoke to the other, "I will build a fire while you find something to eat." Without another word he turned to gather wood from dead trees and limbs that had fallen throughout the years. The other pulled a rifle out of a holster that he had taken off of the mule and soon disappeared into the distance.

After the wood was piled up, the man turned and pulled a roll out of his pack. He unrolled it and there was a pile of matches inside. He removed one and returned the rest to where they were. Then, in a quick swiping motion, he drug the match across the back of his pant leg. There I saw it for the first time, *fire.* He placed the match in some small shavings that he had made with his knife, and they began to burn. On top of that he placed small sticks, dead weeds, and small branches. As they began to burn, he started piling larger pieces on top until the entire pile was on fire.

As the wood burned, the smoke rose through my branches. I could smell the smoke, although it was a new and strange smell, it was bitter sweet. For it was pleasant, but it was made from other trees that I have known in the past. They have laid around and taken years to disappear, but once thrown into the flames, they were gone in a matter of minutes.

At that moment I was startled by a loud bang. It was a sound that I had never heard before, but one that I would come to hear much too often, the sound of a gun. Minutes later, the other man returned with a rabbit. Without any words, one man put a pan on the fire, and the other man walked to the stream with the rabbit and cleaned it. It was then put into the pan and cooked. This was something deeper than I had ever known before. Years ago, I saw a man drag a deer away, but now I was able to see how it was prepared. The smell that came off of it, mixed with the smoke of the fire, was pleasant. I felt ashamed as if I had betrayed my kind for the fire, or nature for the animals.

After the food was eaten and night had fallen, both men leaned against me as they sat on the ground and watched the fire. One of the men pulled a harmonica out of his pocket and began to play. Oh, what a wonderful sound it made, I had never heard anything to compare. The notes sounded as if they had been practiced by the fire for a long time, for it seemed as if the flickering of the fire kept perfect timing with the music being played as a ballerina would dance to music across the dance floor.

As the music eventually faded so did the fire. They slid down and pulled the skins across them and went to sleep. I watched as they slept throughout the night,

mumbling ever so often. As I watched them, I wondered if I would ever see man again. There must not
be many of them for in sixty years I have only encoun-
tered them twice. Both times were so dramatic, and
they brought out feelings that I did not know existed.

Morning came. As the sun rose, so did they. As
they disappeared into the distance, I was left wondering, for the first time, what it would be like to be
able to move from place to place. But, of course, I
would never know. For I am just a tree, and I just stood
there. I watched and listened, for I could not move.

Chapter Five

First Glimpse Of Love

*L*ife in the forest continues, for the most part a repeat of the day before and the year before and so on. But lately, things have been changing. In the last ten years I have seen man many more times. Most of these times they were just passing by. Mostly walking beside the stream or at least in view of it. I cannot tell if they use it as a marking on nature's map or they simply feel the need to stay close to the water. For water, and the need of it is one thing that man and trees have in common. We have had dry years where the rain was not as plentiful as in other years. The ground would become dry and, in a panic, my roots would start to grow down toward any moisture that was beneath me until my thirst was quenched.

However, this year was a good year. Not only was the rain plentiful, but man revealed a secret that was kept from me for the eighty years of my life.

As I was dancing with the wind one afternoon, just like in the past I heard a noise in the distance and then saw man approaching. Just like in the past, I was anxious to see what new experience, good or bad, I would have. This time, however, I saw three humans and a horse. Two were close in size but the other one was smaller. This must be a child. He wore a deerskin cloth around his middle and he had moccasins on his feet. This was my first time seeing a child. Although I would learn many things from man in my life, the things I would learn from children were of greater value and would bring me much more happiness. Unlike man, when a child would work at his chores he would find time to play and smile. And if you look with your heart, the smile of a child is a strong, infectious thing.

As I stood thinking about the child, I also saw a difference in the other man. For it was not a man at all, but it was a woman. As they walked up to me, they stopped and began taking things down from the horse and set up camp. And just as many others who have stopped, one starts a fire and the other searches for food. As the man left with his bow, the woman and child began gathering wood. As I watched the woman, I could see a difference in her face from the man's. There was a beauty that compared to flowers and other things that are pleasant to look upon. When she walked, bent over to gather wood, or to just drop it in a pile, it was with a graceful motion that would not be matched by any other female animal that I have ever seen.

Shortly after the man left, he returned with meat from the hunt. As the woman prepared the food, the father and the boy went down to the stream. The father began to skip rocks across the water. After a few times the boy began to try and after several failed attempts, the father knelt down beside the boy and with one arm around his waist and the other on his hand, he demonstrated the proper level and angle to make a perfect skip. It was an interaction that I had never seen before. For I have seen mother animals playing with their young, but never a father. There must be something special about the human race. To see a man and his child interact left strange desires that I have never felt.

Being a tree, I never had a father, but if I could have, it would have been a wonderful experience.

When the food was cooked, the woman called them to eat. They sat in a small circle and would talk and laugh as they pulled the meat off of the stick to eat it. When they were finished with their meal, the man leaned against me, the woman leaned against him, and the child sat on her lap. The man would touch her long black hair, and then with the back of his hand he would stroke her cheek and she would hug her son and he would smile. Not only could you see that these people loved each other, but the love was so strong that you could almost feel it. A family, oh how wonderful it must be to be a part of something so strong. For this people revealed a secret of love for a family to me. But it was obvious that it was no secret to them. But of course I will never know, because I am just a tree, so I just stood there. I watched and listened, for I could not move

Chapter Six

Man Settles Down

*S*ounds are things that I hear when someone or something is coming. It is the song of the wolf and crickets at night. But as time goes by, I can hear new sounds in the distance. But I do not know what they are. When the gentle wind is blowing toward me, I can hear the voice of man as it is carried on the wind. As time goes on, it gets closer and closer until at last, it reaches me.

As I was listening one afternoon, I could hear the sound of a horse pulling a wagon. I had seen one pass by before, and figured that this one would do the same. It took some time before it came into sight but instead of passing, it stopped. There was a woman driving, and a man and his two sons walking in front. They were moving dead limbs and cutting small brush out of the way to make a trail for the wagon to get through.

The woman tied the reins to a handbrake, and the man helped her down. He looked around and said "this looks like a good, rich, level spot. There is a lot of good timber for a house and a barn and there is water in that stream." Without delay, they unhitched the wagon and began to set up camp. Just as before, they began with the firewood. But instead of hunting, they put on a pot of beans for food. This was different, for I thought something had to die for man to eat. Maybe there is more that I might learn if I remain long enough on this earth. In the last 100 years I have learned with every new experience that I have had. Anyhow, the day went by, and night came. As before, I watched as they ate, and I watched as they slept, and I watched as they left. However, this time was different. Instead of leaving, they woke up and began to work. They started by cutting small brush, and then came the crosscut-saw. As they started pulling back and forth on the base of a pine tree that had been standing beside me for 50 years or so, I realized that this is the sound that I have been hearing in the distance. And as soon as my friend fell, I found out what the loud cracking and crashing sound was. For man was once again making a call on what would live and what would not. And just as he went, most of my friends did also. And once again, I was spared.

As the days turned into weeks, the logs turned into a cabin. And the part of a forest that I have loved for over 100 years turned into a field.

I went through many emotions as I watched this family from the time they arrived until now. First, I was amazed at their staying. Next, I faced fear, for I never knew if I was next to be cut down. Then, there was sadness as I looked upon the cabin that was made with trees that I had known for so long. To the humans, it was a shelter, a place to keep them safe and warm. To me, it was a monument, standing to remember those that I knew. But in some strange way, it felt as even in death they were stacked together for some greater purpose. And I realized that each log laid by itself was a waste. But when they had all worked together, they became something greater than an individual, they became a home.

Each day I learn so much. I have seen man and, by himself just as I, seem alone. But when they come together as a family, no matter how hard they work, there is a certain peace in being able to rely on each other. And man, just as a log, is a waste until more than one work together to build a family and a home.

The days are getting shorter, and my leaves are a golden brown color. As I close my eyes to sleep this winter, I am left wondering. Will I still be here in the spring, or will I be cut down as I sleep? And if I am, will I become a part of something that will be greater than me by myself?

I may never know, for I am just a tree, so I just stood there. I just watched and listened, for I could not move.

Chapter Seven

A "Civil" War

*L*ife has changed in the past seven years. For I am on the edge of a forest on one side and a field on the other. I have seen the beginning of civilization in its rustic form; from a covered wagon to a log cabin. I have seen man clear the land around me. They have plowed the field and planted corn and vegetables. I have watched as they have harvested and stored them. After all these years of watching man, I realized that we both have advantages and disadvantages. As for me, I do not have to work hard all day or kill animals to eat. I can sit in this one spot and get everything that I need from the ground that is around me. But I am connected to the ground. I cannot travel to go in search of my dreams or to flee out of harm's way. If I am in the sun I cannot find shade. If I am cold I cannot seek out a warm place. I must accept who, where, and what I am. The same is true for man. To be able to chose and move, they must toil from sunup to sundown. In a way, I guess, we are the same. If we are to truly survive, we must stay rooted where we are. For in the past I have watched as man uprooted trees to clear land. It is never a positive thing, for one must give way for others to make way.

Today I realized man's authority over himself and his ruthless attempt to rule others. In the distance I could hear gunshots and canon fire. It was faint and I knew it was miles away from me, but in order for shots to be heard there had to be someone shooting. This is never positive, for it would still affect someone or something somewhere.

After a few days, the shooting stopped. But, little did I know, that I would still see the effects of it. The next day, I heard an approaching noise that I had never heard before. It was a combination of many smaller noises. In the distance, it sounded like a tired hum. But as it got closer, it sounded like the rhythm of a drum beat combined with sad music and melody to create a song of a soldier's march. And as it reached the edge of the field I saw that that was exactly what it was. It was a large group of soldiers that numbered four to five hundred men. They had been victorious in battle in the Civil War. If a true victory can actually be claimed when a nation fights against itself. For even in victory you could see the defeat in their eyes and actions. Their victory song was mixed with tears and sobs. As grown men cried, not only in pain of their wounds, but also in realization that they were at war with each other. Brother against brother, father against son, and countrymen against countrymen.

The men were searching for a place to make camp for the night. The man on the horse rode up to the cabin to inform them of their intentions. The men that were carrying the wounded put them down by the stream to give them water and check their wounds.

Their bodies were tired from fighting and walking. They were hungry and thirsty. They were lonesome and missed their families. For if this is victory, defeat must truly be awful.

As I watched through the night, men would wake up and scream. While others next to them being so tired would not even move. As morning came, the bugle sounded and everyone woke up. Some of the wounded men who went to sleep that night did not wake up the next morning. The same way many old trees in the spring would not wake up from their winter rest.

The dead men were buried beneath trees and the stones were stacked in no particular order to mark their grave. The soldiers fell into line, picked up their wounded and left. When they were gone, I was left with a feeling of sympathy and confusion. In the past, I have seen man and have been amazed by the many things that he has done to survive. From hunting to growing food and building a home. I have been amazed by the many things that he can accomplish when he really puts his mind to it. But when man tries to accomplish something positive with so much death and destruction with no respect for one another, it leaves me wondering how long man will last, if they can't at least consider one another.

In the past I have thought how wonderful it must be to be able to move and interact with someone else, to be able to go places and build things. But if war is a part of man, then I am blessed to be a tree. So, I just stood there, I watched and listened for I could not move.

Chapter Eight

A Steam Engine

*W*hat a beautiful sunrise. I stand wondering how many years that I have been able to watch the sun as it slowly creeps over the mountain. Like a small child climbing from behind a log. For when I was in the forest my view was blocked by other trees. The beauty of a sunrise was not missed, for I never truly saw one until my friends were cut down. I would never have traded beauty for friendship, but since I had no choice, I am grateful for at least a beautiful sunrise to mark where they stood.

I have been here for one hundred and forty-three years. It has been thirty-five years since my home was transformed to a field with a cabin. The cabin has been gone now for a few years, and with it, the monument to my friends that it represented. In its place stands a house that was made from boards that was sawed from trees that I have never seen. There are also other houses that have sprung up around me and the field that used to be forest is now a small town. In the past year they have been building a railroad. In the distance I can see it hanging along the side of a mountain like garland around a Christmas tree.

Then my thoughts as well as my silence were broken by a strange noise. It, like many others, was one that I have never heard before and will never forget. In the past I existed in a world where man and animal walked and crawled and in my amazement, I saw the technology of a horse and wagon. Who would have ever thought of something so awesome. Then I felt the ground tremble and a whistle that cut through the hills like a sharp ax through a young sapling. I saw a line of black smoke rising above the trees in the distance. As it came around the last bend of the mountain, I saw it for the first time. A steam engine. Even at such a great distance, it looked huge. Each time that I think that I have seen everything there is to see, something new comes along and lets me know that I should not set a limit on man's ability to create or adapt. For this piece of steel was not alive, but it was fed coal, straight into its fiery belly and drank water. It was converted to power that was so strong it had to be contained by steel tracks and it's appetite so huge, that it pulled a car of coal behind it. It did not need horses to pull it, for the power it created was for its motion. But it was not alive and it was not dead, it just existed.

As weeks and months passed, the railroad was finished and the steam engine began to move back and forth each day. With each trip, it would stay away longer and longer. It was hauling coal that was being mined out of the mountain. And it seemed, as with my early experience with man, it would come and go but I did not know where it went. As I stood watching the sun go down, I wondered how many sunsets I have left. I have been here so long that I have seen man and trees come and go and I still stand here. I have grown tall and straight. I have gained knowledge that I will never be able to use. For I am just a tree, I will never create anything. I will never teach anyone anything and I will never be anything more than a tree. But even if I have knowledge that I will never use, at least I will have something. There are many who have the ability to learn and create and they will never use it. No matter how long they have, their life will be a waste. At least I have knowledge, so I just stood there, proud. I watched and listened, for I could not move.

Chapter Nine

A Man Named Tom

*I*n the ten years since the railroad was built, the little town has grown larger. It seems like everyone comes to work in the coalmine. The people have children and then the children grow up and work in the coalmine and no one really moves away. It seems like men and trees are so similar in life but so different in shape. When acorns fall from a tree, other trees spring up around it and it eventually becomes a forest. The only way an acorn leaves is if it rolls down the hill or falls into the creek. When man increases it is called a town, but when they leave it is in search of something different and it is by choice. This is unlike the acorn, who has no choice when it falls into the creek.

There is a young man that lives in the house where the cabin stood. I have watched him grow from a small child into a young man. I have seen his toys change as well as his attitude. There is something about this young man that has always seemed different. He has always been kind to everyone and everything that was around him. His father would leave early to go to work in an office at the mine and would come back just as it was getting dark each day.

His mother would walk him to school each morning until he finally convinced her that he was old enough to go by himself. I remember the strange look on her face as she let go of his hand.

With a quick wave of his hand, he was off on his own. As he rounded the corner, his mother came and sat under me. She must have cried for an hour. Without a word, she dried her tears and started going about her daily chores. Every so often she would glance to the corner where she last saw him, until he returned home later that day. Running up to his mother, with a look of great accomplishment, he yelled "I did it Mom, all the way there and back. All by myself."

"Yes Tommy, I knew you could do it. I wasn't worried at all." With that, she knelt down and hugged him as if he had been gone for years. As time went on, each day it was a little easier to let him go. But each day she would still look back to the corner waiting for his return with the same anticipation as the day, week, and month before. I was touched with the emotion that I felt. I wanted to laugh, cry, or shout but I could not, for I am just a tree. In the past I saw pleasant things and wondered what it would be like to experience them. But then I saw the pain of war and the results of misunderstandings between men, and I was glad to be a tree. However, the love that I have seen between this family for each other cannot be explained by a tree. For if I had a chance to experience the true love like I have seen between this mother and child, I would take my chances on war or anything else. If man could just understand how it would feel to be a tree, and not be able to experience love or use the vast knowledge that you have gained, they would understand how important love and knowledge really is.

I am glad, however, that Tommy was able to appreciate his experience. Tommy has now finished school and has gone to work with his dad at the coalmine.

Tommy, who is now twenty years old and introduces himself as Tom, has met a young lady. When they walk by, holding hands, or just sit, talking, I can see a glow in their eyes that tell they are looking deeper into each other than their faces. Their souls are opened to each other.

The respect that Tom has for Melinda is evident in his voice and his actions. They have never kissed or even hugged. The respect for each other and the control over their emotions was learned from their parents. A lesson well learned.

Chapter Ten

The Gift Of Me

*T*om and Melinda have been dating for a year now and are planning on getting married. Tom's father has given him a small piece of ground by the stream, about five hundred yards from where I stand. He has been building a small house for him and Melinda to move into after they are married. He has worked on it for over four months now. He and his father work on it in the evenings, after work, and on the weekends. I have seen man work all around me for years now and at the end of each day I can see that they are tired and worn out. It is shown by their partially slumped bodies and a look of exhaustion on their faces. But Tom shows up after a full day of work at the mine all bright-eyed and works well into the night. It seems that he is working on an energy that comes from within that is fueled by dreams of hope that he has set in his mind to accomplish. Whether he will achieve them or not is up to him. If I were a betting man, instead of a tree, my money would be on his success. For even as a child, from riding a bicycle to learning how to skate, when he fell he would get back up and start again.

I have been around long enough to see people give up on many things, but never Tom.

As they were working on Tom's house one evening, a man came by to talk to Tom's father. The two men walked right up to me. Tom's father said, "Tom and Melinda will be married in a few months and I wanted to give them something special for their wedding gift. I was wanting your opinion on this tree."

The other man replied, "This tree is tall and straight. There are no lower limb scars on it, and it would leave a wonderful wood grain and would be large enough to do the job. If it is okay, I will start in the morning."

As they turned and walked away, I was left wondering what they possibly meant. I guess I really knew, deep in my heart, what it was about, but if I played stupid, it might go away. As night fell, reality started to creep back in. My memories drifted back to when I was an acorn in the squirrel's mouth. I knew that that was the end of me, but to my surprise, it turned out to be a new beginning. For when the squirrel forgot where I was buried, and nature took over, I was transformed into a tree. Maybe, by some chance, the same fate or luck will befall me again. But I do not know how. For years I have watched as other trees have been cut down, and they stood there, helpless, as the saw or the ax would cut into them, and as soon as they fell, they were gone.

I stood all night thinking about how much time I had left. I have stood here for one hundred and sixty-nine years. And now it seems that my time is measured in the span of hours instead of years. For man has made a call, once again, and this time, it affects me.

This time tomorrow, I will be history. I have no control over my outcome. The only chance that I have for anything positive to come from me is for someone to consider the shape that I have grown in the time that I have been here. Will I become toothpicks or a great wooden pedestal?

Chapter Eleven

The End Of An Era

*D*aybreak came much too soon. And so did a group of men with mules and a wagon. They were greeted by Tom and his father on their way to work as if nothing would be lost.

It is sad that man could not at least show a little bit of appreciation for something that took one hundred and sixty nine years to grow. Some sign of sympathy would have been better than nothing. But I was just a tree. I will take with me the knowledge that I have gained and I will be proud of who I was while I was here. As I was thinking, my hours turned into minutes. Two men walked up to me with a saw. Each man spat into his hands then laid the saw to my trunk. I could feel the pain as the saw was pulled back and forth. I could see small chips of myself, that were important to me, just fall to the ground to be discarded. I began to cry in pain and total defeat, but no one could hear me, for I was just a tree. I knew that my time was close at hand and anything that I wanted to do had better be done quickly. So I did the only thing that I could; I looked and listened. Over the grinding of the saw I could still here the birds sing. As I looked up I saw the mountains in the distance and the beauty of it all. That is where my eyes remained.

With each pass of the saw goes another inch of my life. Now this large, massive shape that I have taken, which in the past has been my strength against strong winds, leaves me fearing the gentle breeze that used to rustle my leaves. As they cut nearly through my trunk I hear a crack and my whole world gives way. I feel motion for the first time since I was an acorn. Crashing down between other trees that were around me, I tried to reach out and grab them but I could not, for I am just a tree. And as I hit the ground for the first time in one hundred and sixty nine years, I am no longer a tree. Now I am just a log with limbs, and as the men with axes approach, it won't be long until I am just a log.

As I lay on the ground and my limbs are piled up, I do not know what to expect next. For I can remember the deer and how, once he fell, it did not take him long to die. But I could not feel any difference, other than the position that I lay. There is pain and humiliation, but I do not feel death. Maybe it takes trees longer to die than it takes a deer.

As I am waiting to see what happens, I am rolled upon a wagon. Chains are put across me to hold me in place and my journey begins. I look around but no longer can I see the mountains, all I see are trees and houses.

As the mules start to pull the wagon, I can feel the jerk when the harness tightens around their necks. As the wagon rolls, I can feel each bump as the solid wooden wheels go through the ditch along the road. It is a bumpy ride, but it is the first ride that I have ever taken. As I was pulled along the road, for the first time in my life I was mobile. I could not walk, but I was traveling. My journey was a little over two miles and it took the mules a little over two hours to get me to my destination. But, when you stand in one spot for one hundred and sixty nine years two miles is a great journey. It just happened to end at a sawmill. As I was pulled into the yard, I could see other logs stacked in piles. They looked as if they were prisoners on death row awaiting execution, but there was no life in them and just as the deer, they were gone. How could I not be dead? I feel just as strong and alive as ever. I have felt great pain but it has ceased and I am still alive. There must be more for me to learn before I go. However long that that will take I will listen and I will watch, but I am no longer a tree.

As the wagon stops beside a building, a man comes out and paints the bottom of my trunk where I was cut down with red paint. As the wet paint was applied I remember the blood that stained my bark from the hunter's hand even after he was gone. The blood stayed for weeks to remind me of my experience.

After a few minutes I was pulled ahead and rolled off on steel rollers. As the wagon pulled away I could see a man shoveling coal into a furnace under a steam engine that was connected to a saw mill. As one man started pushing me ahead another man grabbed a large lever, and when he pulled it, the large blade on the saw started to spin. As it got faster it's sharp teeth cut through the air and made a whistling sound until the blade started hitting my wood. As I was pushed through, I could feel the cold steel blade as it sliced through me. I knew that if I was not dead

I soon would be. Each time I was pushed through another slice was taken off. When the saw stopped, I was just a pile of boards stacked neatly in a pile. On the end of each board was the red paint to mark all the boards for Tom's dad, but I was still there. I was not dead, but I was a stack of boards.

Chapter Twelve

A New Life

A stack of boards marked with red paint. I would have never dreamed that I could come this far and still be alive, or whatever I am.

I have been stacked in the sun for two weeks now. A process called air drying, where the sun shines down on me and the wind blows across and all of the moisture in me is dried out. Life is different. When I was tree during dry months I would suck as much water as possible from the soil and still not have enough at times. But now as it evaporates, I am okay. I guess water is something that a board does not need.

People have been passing by and talking about a nice wood grain as they would flip me over to further the drying process.

I was wondering what would happen next. Would I become a part of Tom's house or what? Just then I heard a wagon pull up and it was Tom's dad. Tom was not with him, but there were other men to help him load this stack of boards that I have become. As soon as I was loaded I was on my second journey. I can feel the jerks of the horses and bumps in the road but I cannot see where I am going because of the sides of the wagon. They, too, are just boards, but they are dead. I cannot understand my existence. For animal as well as trees when they are dead they no longer exist, but for some reason I do. Maybe I will find out at the end of this journey.

This time my ride was not as long. Ten minutes after it started, it was over. I was unloaded inside of a building. This was the first time that I have ever been inside any building. Tom's dad asked an old man with a long beard how long it would take to make the suite. "Oh, just holler back in about three weeks," answered the man with the beard.

In no time at all Tom's dad was back in the wagon and gone.

I was all alone inside a dark building and night was falling. With the little light that was left from the sunset I could see different types of tools and work benches around the room. On the floor were piles of sawdust and the smell of cedar was evident in the building. In the back were pieces of furniture that looked as if they were not completely assembled. I realized that this was a place that made furniture and I guessed that was what I would become.

As night gave way to morning, the two large wooden doors of the building were opened. In walked the old man with the long beard and his two sons. "We need to get started on Tommy's set right off" he said.

As soon as it was said, they started grabbing my boards and laying me on a work bench sorting different boards for different things. When they were finished they had three piles, "these for the bed, these for the chest of drawers, and these for the dresser."

As the sons were laying out the tools that they would need the old man was telling them that they had to do a special job on this set. It was a special wedding present for Little Tommy and his wife that Tommy's dad had been planning for a long time. Without another word they began to work. They began by measuring and marking on me. Then came the hand saw, it was not as large and scary as a crosscut, but it was still a saw.

As I was yet cut into smaller pieces and placed into different piles some of me was discarded and my sawdust was just swept into a pile with the rest. Then came the planer. The rough surface that the saw-mill blade left was planed smooth. Then there were pieces of me clamped to the table and the younger of the two brothers started to work with the wood chisel. As I watched them work it was like nothing I had ever seen. From log cabins to houses and barns and wagons that were built that looked so well. But these boys were artists. They took time to measure, fit, and sand everything. And when they were finished, you could tell, they did not build anything, instead they created art out of wood.

Days turned into weeks and the pile of lumber that I was, was transformed into a beautiful bedroom suite. As I looked at the chest and dresser I could see the effort put in them. And with the coat of varnish it had a finish and a shine that would compare to nothing that I had ever seen and... and...

I just realized that I am a bed. For some reason, I am not a dresser or a chest of drawers. I am a bed. I can see the chest and dresser that was made from a part of me, but I can't feel them. All my memory and all the knowledge that I have gained is in me. A bed. Not an acorn, not a tree. But a bed.

At that time I did not know how important a bed really was. But I came to find out that man spends 1/3 of his life in bed. Some of the greatest memories and some of the saddest moments will be in a bed. And though I will support them through it all, they will never appreciate me for it. For I am now just a bed. So I looked and listened, for I could not move.

Chapter Thirteen

The Wedding Gift

*A*s I was loaded onto a wagon for the third time, for some reason, I was handled with more care than ever before. Blankets were wrapped around me and ropes were laid across me with care. The route that the wagon had taken was a lot smoother than the other times. I could not see for the blankets around me. I could hear many things on our trip home. We passed a school and I could hear children laughing. I could hear the squeaking of the seesaw and I wished so much to be able to see the smiles of the children. In the past I have become addicted to the happiness of children. It is something that no matter how often or how long you see it, you anxiously look forward to next time. For the smile of a happy child is more grand than any sunrise and the sound of their laughter is sweeter than the most beautiful birdsongs.

As we went along, the laughs were muffled by distance and then were completely silenced by the sound of the train as it made its morning run. And then we were home.

As the blankets were pulled off of me I could see that we were at Tom's house. In the four or five weeks that I was gone, he had made a lot of progress. It looked as if everything was done. The only thing left to do was to put the furniture in and here I was. As they began unloading the dresser I looked to see the place where I stood for so long and the only thing that was left was a stump and a pile of ashes were my limbs and everything else that was left was burned.

My foundation, my history, and my place in life for 169 years now consists of a partially burnt stump and a pile of ashes. I am left with a feeling of sorrow. I suppose I feel as a quadriplegic might. For even if you have lost the use of your limbs if you still have your limbs, there is still hope. Hope that maybe something will change, but after they are gone so is any hope for a cure. So now I will be what I was made to be. From what I have made of myself that I was, for now I am just a bed.

As soon as the chest and dresser were brought in, so was I. After Tom's dad had placed a thick cotton mattress on me, Tom's mother placed white sheets and a light blue bed spread on the mattress. Minutes later, Tom and Melinda walked in. All four stood silent for a moment just looking at what was made of me. Melinda broke the silence, saying, "It is just beautiful. I love it so very much."

Tom just turned and hugged his dad and with a tear in his eye, said, "Thank you, dad, this means so much to Melinda and I. Thanks Mom."

"It is something your mom and I wanted to do for years," said his dad. "My father had the bedroom suite made that your mother and I had for a wedding gift. It meant so much to us that we thought that we would give you the same gift and hoped it meant as much to you."

For years I had thought that I was an attractive tree. People had passed by and looked at me but I have been a bed for only a few days and people smile and say how beautiful I am. Just the sight of me has made man show emotion about me that I have seen only between them and their children. My desires have been to experience love and feel needed. For some reason, my prayers are being answered. Though I cannot return emotions to them physically, it makes me so happy. For true love is about needing and being needed and giving whatever is needed. And they must have needed a bed. So finally I am loved.

As darkness fell, they closed the windows that the breeze blew through and shut the doors. Tom's father patted him on the shoulder and said, "Well, just two more days and you will be an old married man." They laughed and disappeared into the distance. I was a bed, so I watched and listened for I could not move. But, I felt that I was loved.

Chapter Fourteen

Life In A Home

Sunrise looks different through a window pane. In the past I was outside being a part of it all. The birds that were singing were sitting upon my branches and I was the tree that left the early morning shadows on the ground. Life, now, will be different. Instead of being a part of the sunrise, I will now have to watch it through a window. I do not know what to expect. Nor do I know how I will feel or how long I will last. Will I make a difference? I have time and I guess time will answer all of my questions, if I look and listen. I have learned much as a tree. I have gained many desires over the years. Now I feel that I may have a chance to experience more than ever before.

Today is Tom and Melinda's big day. It is about 4:00 PM and I just heard the church bells ringing. I do not know if that means that it is the beginning or the ending of the wedding, but I do know that it means that tonight I will be spending my first night with my new family. I am anxious to see how people act inside houses and what goes on in them. All I know is that man spends a lot of time building them and taking care of them. Then they leave early in the morning, work all day, then don't get home until late at night. They seem to be content with this as long as their wife and children have a place to call home. This must be an act of love that can be shown only by a real man and a true father.

As evening falls, I hear a carriage pull up outside. Minutes later I hear a commotion coming through the door. When the door is opened I can see Tom as he carries his new bride across the threshold of their new home. He carries her across the room and, before he puts her down, recites what sounds to be a personal vow to her. "Melinda, I will always honor the vows for better or worse to you as my wife. But as my friend and my soul mate I would like to present to you as a gift, this house. May it always keep us and our future children safe and warm and be more than just a shelter from rain. A place where we can grow and learn the true meaning of love, one to another and pass it along to our children. And as I hold you in my arms, I show you our house. And as your feet touch the floor, I christen it "Our Home." As he put her down in front of the fireplace, she turned and hugged him and through her tears of joy and happiness came a soft whisper, "Thank you for loving me and thank you for our home."

After a long embrace and a short kiss they turned and knelt in front of the fireplace, side by side. Together they started the first fire in the fireplace.

I do not know why I am so lucky as to be part of something so wonderful. I know that I will never be as a family member, or even anything special. As I look around, I see other objects such as chairs and a table, a nightstand with an oil lamp on it, and a broom in the corner. Just as they are, I too, am just an object. But I count myself grateful to be an object in this home. As evening turns into night, their time is being spent talking of their dreams and what they wanted as children and what their names could be. This is the first time that they have discussed this. Before they were married it would not have been appropriate for them to discuss such things. Whether it was out of pure respect for each other, or they were just too shy. But now that they are married, they are finding that they no longer have individual dreams. Their vows, not only united their lives, but their dreams as well.

As the fire faded into coals, they retired into the bedroom. Both of them seemed very nervous and withdrawn. They knelt side by side and said a prayer. They asked for wisdom and guidance and for help to do something that they had never done.

As they laid on the soft, cotton mattress, I witnessed two young adults become husband and wife. I saw an expression of love and the conception of new life. Which, just as I, would become part of this family. As morning came, Tom was awakened by the smell of fresh coffee, as Melinda served his first cup in bed. It was followed by a burst of frying bacon and hot biscuits. I do not know how man can stand so much of so many good things. I do not know how these things taste. But as I laid there that morning, just as I would for thousands of mornings to come, thinking that if I would have died at that moment it would have been okay. For I had smelled heaven and I was ready to go there.

As Tom finished his breakfast, Melinda handed him a small basket of food for his lunch. With a hug and a small kiss, he turned and left for work. Melinda stands by the door and watches Tom walk to and disappear around the same corner that his mother did so many years ago. As she closes the door and turns around I can see tears in her eyes. I cannot understand her tears. Years ago, Tom's mother had cried when he had rounded that corner. Her tears was from the understanding that her life was changing and she knew that she had to let go and give something up in order for Tom to gain something. But Melinda's tears seemed to be a mirror image of his mother's reasons. The things that she had to give up and let go of was the things that made Tom the man that he is today. And the man that he has become is given to Melinda to love, honor, and cherish.

As she sits down upon me, I can feel her mixed emotion. She is so happy that she has started a new life, but she is scared because everything is different.

As I would find many times to come, that change, no matter how big or small, good or bad, would always give way to a certain uneasiness in man. But with time, just as a hole in a belt can be adjusted to make any situation become part of everyday life. And as I, myself, found the most important thing that is overlooked by man is that thing called time. It is not medicine, but it can heal wounds. It has no size, but it is larger than us all. It is not an enemy, but with knowledge and true direction in our lives we will defeat it.

Chapter Fifteen

The Miracle Of Birth

Shortly after Tom and Melinda were married, Melinda started waking up sick. Soon after that I started noticing changes in her body and her moods. Her stomach was growing, just as a deer who is with young. But unlike deer she would be happy laughing and then cry about the same thing only seconds later. I could see how her beautiful, outlined face with each month that would pass would become a little more drained. The energy that it took away from her body, mentally and physically, to create a new life was evident. But overall there was a certain glow about her that seemed as if a happy sign were painted on her forehead.

Tom began working on a small cradle that he sat beside me when it was finished. Melinda made a small mattress that she put in the bottom of the cradle. Her days were filled with sewing and knitting. The small gowns and blankets that she made began to fill a chest that was set at the foot of the bed that I had become. It seemed that the new life that was being made inside of Melinda was important enough to alter everyday life in preparation for its arrival. Everything that was being done was placed around me. I was not the center of attention, but it was as if I was on the front row seat of a theatrical production. The "Creation Of Life" was being performed right in front of me. I am grateful to see how mankind lives.

For years I have seen man and wondered how his life began and how he learned and what was important to him. For their actions are so diverse. There are some who have seemed evil or else acting in despair which has filled me with fear and uncertainty. There have been those who have just triggered no feeling at all except maybe wonder. And then there have been those who passed by who have shown some act of kindness or charity to someone or something that has left me wondering. Why, if some can be so good and kind, why would others want to waste their lives being so negative.

One evening Melinda was preparing dinner so that it would be done for Tom when he got home from work. She had reached under the cabinet to get a large, black iron pot to place on the wood stove that she already had lit. As she lifted the pot to the stove, her water broke. In a hurry, she placed the pot on the stove and started to clean herself and the floor. Before her task was complete she stopped and let go of the rag that was in her hand. She dropped to her knees and grabbed her stomach and realized that cleaning would have to wait. Her labor had started and her child would not wait. As her first pain let up she ran to the door. In the distance she could see Tom's mother hanging clothes out to dry and began to holler to get her attention. After sending for the doctor, Tom's mother came to assist Melinda. She was explaining about preparing dinner for Tom and was still concerned that he would be hungry when he got home. Then, as the second pain hit, dinner began to seem less important than before. Tom's mother helped her to lay down on the cotton mattress. I could feel a variety of things that she was feeling. Her pain was great, but through it all, I could feel her joy. Though her pain was dominant, it would soon be overcome by joy.

It took about an hour for the doctor to get there. As he stepped onto the porch, Tom rounded the corner. When he saw the doctor, he broke into a run and was home in no time. As he and the doctor entered the house, Tom's mother already had clean linens and water boiling. She filled them in on the time that Melinda had been in labor. As Tom knelt down beside Melinda he began to stroke her cheek with the back of his hand and tell her he loved her and how he was sorry for her pain. As she began to scream in pain I could see the tears swelling in Tom's eyes. I could feel so much from Tom towards Melinda. And as he said that he wished he could bear her pain, I knew he meant it. For someone to love another so much that he would work all day for them to have food and a place to live and still wish he could take her pain was, to this time, the greatest act of love that I have ever witnessed. In turn, I felt that if Melinda could have transferred the pain, she wouldn't have. She would never have wanted him to go through what she was feeling. As the doctor pushed Tom out of the room, he closed the door and said that it was time.

Tom's father had just came in, so Tom and his father waited there together for what seemed to Tom to be days was only about thirty minutes.

As for me, I had a chance to witness the birth of a human being. I saw the head and then came part of the neck. Tom's mother was holding her hand and telling her to push. When the shoulders out, the rest of the baby just squirted out like the juice of an orange. As the baby laid on her mattress, the doctor began to wipe out his eyes and mouth. And just as man grabs a pair of boots, the doctor grabs the baby by the feet and dangles him upside down. With a quick smack across the butt, the child gasps for air and begins to cry. In seconds, the doctor ties a string around the umbilical cord and it is cut. And I realized that Tom and Melinda that had now become three.

Next, Melinda is cared for and the child is cleaned up and dressed in a special gown that was made just for this special day. Tom and his father could now enter the room. There is a glow on Tom's face that I had never seen before. When a man receives a gift, it makes him happy. But when a man receives a child, it is truly a life changing experience. For a child is a gift that when they are born, you must start working on them and never stop. The values that you instill in them, whether they be good or bad, will be reflected in their actions for the rest of their lives.

As Tom takes his child and holds him, there is a connection made that will never be broken. For Tom's father taught him to love and as Tom holds his new son it is evident. "Hello, Lil' Tom, I'm your daddy. I've been waiting for you my whole life."

Chapter Sixteen

A Sick Child

Tom and Melinda had always been happy, but after the birth of Lil' Tom, it seemed as if the sun rose a little earlier each morning. Lord knows Lil' Tom did. And no matter what time it was Melinda was up and taking care of him with a smile that would match any sunrise. Tom would roll over and ask if he could help. "No," said Melinda, "Not unless you can breast-feed him. If not go back to sleep so you can go to work after while."

It is really something the way that love works. No matter what people have, no matter if it is food or anything else, when they share it, each person gets half. And when another person comes along each person only gets a third. But with love, when another comes along, each person gets the whole thing. For love, when it is shared, it always increases.

As time passed, love seemed to increase. Each time Lil' Tom would learn something new, there would be an increase in happiness. First came a smile that would nearly burst into a laugh. And then he found that he had control his hands and would try to grab every-thing. Then he began to sit up. Then to crawl and then to walk. Each time he would accomplish a goal, you could see pride in Tom and Melinda's smiles.

Tom and Melinda were good parents. You could tell by the amount of time that they would set aside out of a busy day to take with Lil' Tom. From teaching him to walk to caring for him when he was sick. I have never seen any other living creature spend so much time with their young. But then I have never seen any other young that needed so much attention. It must come from what is expected of man. Whereas other animals just expect their young to walk on all fours their entire life, if a child is not walking upright by the age of one, then he is behind. With animals, when the mother chirps, grunts, or snorts, the young knows that it is mom and just does what she does to survive. But man has to learn to talk and understand what is being said. And then, on top of that, they must learn to communicate which seems to be the hardest part. Sometimes you must totally ignore what is being said and try to figure out what the other person wants by reading whatever mood they are in. When an animal seeks shelter, it will dig a hole or live under a tree. Man must spend time building a house and having furniture and still want more. So, I guess if that is what is expected it would probably take longer to teach them what is expected. But it is not only the young who must learn, for when a child is born good parents realizes they know nothing. Then, this love thing comes into play again and works with nature and everything seems to all work out the way it should. To have the ability to learn is a wonderful thing. As hard as some things are to learn it seems the most important thing come easy and are taken for granted and the secondary things are harder to learn but they, too, have a part in life.

Do you remember the first thing that you learned to do when you were born? It was probably the simplest and quickest lesson that you have ever learned and it is the most important thing you will do every day for the rest of your life until the day you die. It is simply to breathe.

The next lesson is eating. It takes most people less than an hour or two. Every living thing is born, hatched, or sprouted with the need and desire to consume something. When something gets poked around your mouth long enough you get the picture and you learn what to do.

Then there are things like math and reading. It is not something you need to survive, it just makes survival so much easier. It takes years to really learn enough to be really useful and the more you learn, the more you realize you will never learn it all.

I feel for some reason that I have been blessed with the ability to learn. I will never read or figure out how to do math, but I have learned about life, death, good and bad. I have seen many things come and go, from man to time, and I will never have control over either. I do not have a body, but I do have a mind.

Therefore I am grateful to be able to learn. I do have control over that and I will use it. I will take the simple things in life and I will not only see them for what they are, but I will see where they have come from. And I will try to see how their past dictates their future and who they can be, if they have learned from their mistakes. I cannot walk, run, holler, or communicate, but if I learn I will not spend my time feeling sorry for myself and what I cannot do, but I will have pride in what I can.

As Lil' Tom turns one, Melinda is expecting another child. Lil' Tom is now sleeping in another room. In the middle of the night, he wakes up crying. Melinda runs to see what was wrong with him and finds that he has a fever. As she carries him into the room, she wakes Tom to help her. If nothing else but for moral support. For when man is in crisis, it helps if they have someone to worry with them. As she lays Lil' Tom on the mattress, I can feel the fever in his little body. Melinda checks his temperature. It is 103 degrees. The first thing that she does is starts to cry. In 1910 there was not an all night drug store to run to get something for fever. High fever has crippled and killed many children in the past. It had to be dealt with, with whatever they had.

In seconds Tom was up and went to the well out-side to draw water. Melinda got a small washtub that she used to bathe him in. In no time at all Tom returned with the water and was out the door again to get the doctor. Melinda filled the tub and placed Lil' Tom in the water to try to cool his temperature. His cries were broken with short spans of shivering and after awhile he became too weak to cry and would just groan every once in awhile between cold chills. It took over an hour for Tom and the doctor to return. Melinda took Lil' Tom out of the water and dried him off and handed him to the doctor. He checked his temperature and found it had went down two degrees because of the cool bath. The doctor checked him out and said that his lungs sounded clear. He reached into his bag and pulled out a small glass bottle with a rubber cork in it. He said "give him a dropper full every couple of hours and do not let him have any milk. He can only have sugar water or juice if you have any. Check his temperature every hour or if he starts to cry or whine. If he gets over 102 degrees, try to cool him down.

Tom and Melinda both stayed up the rest of that night giving him sugar water and the medicine that the doctor had left. Each time his temperature went up they would bathe him in cool water again. This continued until the next evening when his fever finally broke. All three went to sleep that evening and slept all night without waking.

I see that Lil' Tom had the fever but it effected all three people. When a parent loves a child, and the child becomes ill, everything around becomes less important than it was and the only thing that matters is for the child to return to its natural state of health. And when they do, so do their parents.

Three months later, Tom and Melinda had their second child. They named her Elaine. And just as with Lil' Tom, their love multiplied.

Chapter Seventeen

Tough Love, Something To Remember

*A*s the children grew and the years passed I could see a repeat of Tom's mother toward her children in the actions of Melinda. Loving and letting go. It is hard sometimes to let go. For when I was a tree I used to hold the nests of birds. When the mother knew her babies were ready, she would urge them out in her own way. Some would try to fly and with some luck, on the way down, would land on a lower limb. They would flutter around from limb to limb and finally make it back to the nest. Some would make it all the way to the ground and then back up. The weak or lazy would be eaten by predators. I find after watching for a while, that love can also be tough. And tough love is just as nurturing as a gentle hug. For gentle love will build confidence but tough love gives strength to support the confidence that you have gained and one without the other is like drawing water from an empty well, it just doesn't happen.

I had seen the children get spankings from time to time. They were good kids and didn't really get many.

One tough love story that really stands out to me was when Lil' Tom was about twelve years old. One day when he finished his after school chores, he began playing with a group of boys. They were playing baseball in the field next to Lil' Tom's house. A little boy had just recently moved into the neighborhood. He was about the same age as Lil' Tom. All he had on was a worn out pair of overalls. He had on no shirt or shoes. The boy walked over to the fence where the other boys were playing and was trying to build enough courage to speak. He started out with what sounded to be a squeak and then straightened out, "Hey... my name is Lawrence. My paw just moved here to work in the mine. I don't know nobody and I was wonderin' if I can play ball with yawl."

Everyone stood still and got quiet. Finally someone asked him, "why ain't you wearin' any shoes?"

"I ain't got none," said Lawrence. "My paw is supposed to get me some fore winter."

Then one of the boys said, "You ain't got no shoes?" then one of the boys started to snicker, "Well, you best tell your paw to get you a shirt, too."

Then, Lil' Tom, wanting to be part of the group, started to laugh and pick at Lawrence. As he dropped his head in disappointment and turned to walk away, Tom came around the corner from work. As he was walking up he had heard the whole thing.

"Hey, Lawrence, what's happening?"

"Nothing" said Lawrence. "I was just going home."

Tom grabbed him by the shoulder and said, "hang on a minute, ole buddy. I want you to meet my son, Lil' Tom. As they walked back toward the group of boys Tom said, "hey fella's, I would like for you all to meet my friend, Lawrence. He lost his ma in a house fire last year, along with everything they had. He and his dad came to see me about a job last week and I told his dad that if he would let Lawrence go to school I would try to pay him a little more." As Tom stood there beside Lawrence you could not even hear a sound from anyone. "I want you all to know that I am ashamed of all of you. But Lil' Tom, it makes me sad that you would laugh at anyone's misfortune. You owe him an apology."

As Lil' Tom stood there with his head hung low, he said in a small voice, "I'm sorry. And I'm sorry about your ma, too."

As Lil' Tom turned to walk back to the house Tom said, "Wait a minute. We can't have anyone else laughing at Lawrence for not having good clothes. Come back here."

"What?" asked Lil' Tom.

"You look about the same size as Lawrence, strip down to your long johns and let him have yours."

Without a word Lil' Tom slipped out of his shirt and trousers and gave them to Lawrence.

"Hey," said Tom, "the socks and shoes, too." "But these are the only pair I've got," Lil' Tom complained, "What am I gonna do?"

"I don't know," said Tom, "since you're gonna have to start doing twice as many chores, you might get some before winter."

As Lil' Tom walked home in his underwear and bare feet he learned a very tough love lesson that he never forgot. Ever.

As Tom walked into the house, Melinda, who had been standing at the window watching everything, smiled and said, "Wash up, dinner is ready."

Just as all lessons that we learn help us, the "tough love" lessons are the ones that we remember most because of the impact they have on our lives. When Lil' Tom walked back home in his underwear, he was embarrassed. But the true lesson that he learned that day was that everyone has feelings. It goes far beyond clothes or shoes. Lil' Tom and Lawrence became friends. Lil' Tom never forgot how he made Lawrence feel, but Lawrence did.

Chapter Eighteen

Some Things Change, Some Stay The Same

*T*ime keeps on going and as time passes, people get older and things change. I have watched Lil' Tom grow into a young man and insists that he be called Tom or Tom Jr. It is something how when a boy gets to a certain age in his life he starts too feel grown up for innocent or sweet names given to them by their parents in their youth. His father, after years of simple living had saved enough money to send both Tom Jr. and Elaine to college. So, back in the 1930's when they ran electric lines through town, Tom figured he would splurge and get Melinda lights for the first time in her life. They had seen them before but lines had never made their way to the small towns until then. I could see through the window, the long poles that were going up along side of the road and days later they came back and installed the wire. A few weeks later, men came back to install wires in the house. Then, on a cold evening toward the end of that year, Tom walked into the house and asked Melinda if she would like to do the honors. As she flipped a switch on the wall, for the first time I have seen light without fire, and it was good.

More technology has come along. Back in the 1920's Tom bought his first car and now it seems that every year I can see a few more pass by the window. The steam engine they used to haul coal from the mine, now sounds different. Now it runs on diesel and is more powerful and can haul larger loads to help satisfy man's growing need. A few years after electricity was wired into the house, the old, wooden ice box that sat in the kitchen for years gave way to a refrigerator. The old iron that Melinda used to set on the stove was replaced with an electric one. The rub board still hangs on the back porch where she hung it up to dry the last time she used it. It was replaced by a washing machine. The old bucket and dipper that sat on the counter was replaced with a sink and water that comes out of a pipe. Now Tom is talking about putting a toilet inside. So many things have been changing from technology to the way people look and live. The house that is filled with new gadgets is quiet now except for the constant buzz of the refrigerator. The small feet that used to jar the floor as they ran through the house are gone. And now they only show up as occasional visitors on a larger scale.

Tom Jr. and Elaine have married and started their own lives in their own homes. Each have children and they visit often. Tom and Melinda have been married for over 40 years. You can tell by the lines on their faces that they have worked hard their entire lives. You can tell by the smiles on their faces that they have been happy. They have helped each other through thick and thin. There have been more thick times than thin. They have loved and raised their children on love and taught them respect. They were the example that they used to teach them by.

I still enjoy watching Tom and Melinda go to bed every night. After prayers, one will roll back the covers for the other. They hug, and kiss and say 'goodnight'. They snuggle close and go to sleep just as they did that first night, every night. And as so many things change, their love remains the same.

When I was in the forest, I would wonder about man. What were they? Where did they go? And even, what was their purpose for being here? I have not yet had my questions answered. But since I have become a bed and have been moved into their environment, I am impressed with the way they love, learn and adapt to those who are around them.

Chapter Nineteen

Death Of Tom

*T*om has been coughing a lot here lately and each day Melinda tries to talk him into going to see a doctor. But Tom, being blessed with good health most of his life, insists that unless you are needing stitches or having a baby they are just a waste. "I am not a woman, nor am I cut anywhere, I'll be all right."

Tom had retired from the coal mine a few years earlier. After 48 years he figured he would try something different with the rest of his life. And after just a few weeks spending time with his grandchildren and great grandchildren, he figured out what he would do. Seeing that they were in great need of fishing lessons, so between fishing lessons and his garden he has stayed busy.

One morning as he wakes coughing, he begins to notice blood becoming more common. There is pain in his lungs that will not quit. This time when Melinda suggests the doctor, it doesn't seem like such a bad idea. After a few tests and X-rays, the doctor returns with bad news.

"Well, Tom," says the doctor, "You have developed Black Lung. The years of working in and around that mine have caught up with you. Best thing you can do is try to get a lot of rest and don't do any lifting or walking. Avoid anything that would make you breathe heavy. I can give you something for your cough and pain, but you are really past help. Other than trying to stay comfortable, this is the best we can do.

When Tom and Melinda came home, Tom laid down. Melinda just sat beside him holding his hand without saying a word for nearly an hour. I could feel the fear and hopelessness that they were both feeling as Tom rolled on his side. I saw the first tear that I had ever seen in his eyes. "I told you doctors were just a waste." Said Tom.

As the days went by, Tom began to grow weaker. His cough began to worsen. And instead of going to eat at the table, Melinda began to feed and bathe him in bed. When Tom would have the strength to talk, he would try to encourage her. He knew that when he was gone, it would be hard on Melinda. Maybe if he acted like it didn't bother him it would be easier. I could see that he was more concerned about her than he was about dying.

Tom has been a true man his whole life. Even as a child while I was a tree he had seemed to care about everyone and everything before himself. And now, on his death bed he worries about Melinda.

"I have always loved you." Whispered Tom.

Melinda smiled and said, "That's what made it so easy to love you back."

Tom closed his eyes and his breathing started to slow. Soon it became small gasps that came from the back of his throat. And then it stopped. My friend of 74 years was gone.

Melinda laid her face upon his forehead and began to cry. All though Tom Jr. and Elaine were by her side, she was alone for the first time in 53 years.

As Tom had taken his last breath, I could feel the pain and sickness that he had suffered the past few months seem to fall through the mattress and the floor. And from Tom I could sense a cool, calm happiness that seemed to rise from his body. In the distance I could hear voices, but I could not hear the words. I tried to cry out and I tried to grab for him with arms I did not have. For I was just a bed. I could not talk. I could not move.

Chapter Twenty

The Loss Of Melinda

*E*very time I see Melinda sit alone, it is hard for me not to think of Tom. Also, they had been together for so long and depended upon each other for everything from coping with problems to finishing each other's sentences.

It has been ten years since Tom has passed away. Melinda starts each morning with the same routine. As soon as she wakes she kneels besides me and says her prayers. She dresses herself, sits by a picture of Tom and talks to him as if he were sitting next to her. I have seen how this has helped her. In the years past, I have watched her and Tom kneel and pray to someone they have never seen. And this made them happy, and things always seemed to work out. Now the time she spends talking to Tom's picture seems to make her happy and help with the loneliness.

At times I wish she knew that I was more than just an old oak bed. If I could talk, I would console her. If I had arms, I would hold her. I have cared for her and her family since I first knew them. They have taught me love just by my watching the way that they have treated each other. She has a friend that is so close, but she will leave this world someday and never know me as anything more than furniture. It is something how man has so many friends that he will never know, because he is too shy, or too busy, or too angry to just take time to stop and say hello. If he could just take time to stop and look behind the face of a stranger, he could probably see the heart of his best friend. But man so seldom looks.

Tom Jr. and Elaine have both tried to get Melinda to move in with them, but she insists that she stay where she has been her whole life. Her time is filled with grandchildren that want to sleep over and wake up to her wonderful butter-back biscuits and home-made apple butter. And the bedtime stories that she has filled the imagination and heart of four generations with.

Not one was ever scary. Just as her life, her stories were positive. She had never wasted her time with far-fetched fairy tales or horror stories. She had felt that if she would take the time to tell a story that it should be a time used to build hope, and to plant the seeds of great dreams in fresh soil of the young hearts and minds that she loved. She felt that if she told fairy tales, it would breed something that would never happen and dreams that would always fall short of expectation. Her stories were about animals and people who would have a need and would work hard to accomplish what needed to be done for themselves or someone else. They would always end on a happy or positive note.

One evening after a large family reunion, before her family had left, she called them together and wanted to say something to each one. She hugged and kissed every person that was there and as they left, she told them 'goodbye'. And that she would see them tomorrow or the next time they came by.

At 92 she still lived by herself cleaned her house and cooked. Time had slowed the once vibrant woman that she was, but it never took her spirit.

The next morning, after she had dressed herself, she sat to talk to Tom.

"Good morning." She said, as she was rocking back and forth in her rocking chair. As she talked to him her words became more like whispers. There was a pleasant smile on her face. Then the whispers became silent. The squeaking of the rocker stopped. I thought she had fallen to sleep as she had many times before.

Then, in a clear sharp voice that sounded as if she had come across a friend that she had not seen in years she said, "Tom!" As I looked, her body slumped slightly in her chair. I heard what sounded like happy voices in the room, but I could not understand what they said. Then I knew she was gone.

Once again, I felt helpless. I desired to express great sorrow and grief, to scream or to cry. But I could not. For I was just a bed.

As I looked at her sitting in the chair I could see her body, but the house seemed empty. For the person who had made that body special was no longer there. I realized then that there is more to man than what I see. There is something that is put inside of a man when he is created. It is like putting a hand into a glove. All you can see is the glove. The glove does not make the hand, but it is the hand that is inside of it. This thing that is put inside of a man is what makes the body work. It is the part of him that makes him who he is and who he wants to be. It contains love and desires. It contains physical and emotional needs. It is the part of man that learns and controls him and makes him who he is. Whether that is good or bad is up to him.

If he is important enough to himself, he will understand that if he truly can control himself and everything he does, he will love life and everything in it. But if he loses hope or never has a dream he will never know love or respect for himself or anyone else. Then when the body is worn out or becomes too damaged to repair, it is removed, just as the hand from the glove. When it is gone all that is left is the shape of the hand that was within it.

There is a knock on the door. "Grandma?" The voice says. The door slowly opens and again. "Hello, Grandma? It's just me. I came to check on you." It was Tom Jr.'s youngest son, Jonathon. He had become a doctor and on his way to work each day, he would stop and check on his grandmother. He would make sure she had taken her medicine and see if she was all right. But this time as he walked up and put his hand upon her shoulder, he knew that she was not.

In a low tone he said, "Grandma?" As he knelt beside the chair, he took her hand and put it to his cheek. He began to cry and he told her that he was thankful for all that she had done for him as a child. "It was you who filled my heart with hopes and dreams and I will love you forever and a day."

Jonathon turned and rolled back the blankets on the mattress that Melinda had made just the hour before. He placed her in the bed just as a sleeping child and then he called his dad. I realized then that even my prayer was answered. For over the years as Tom and Melinda prayed, they asked for different things. My prayer was just to hold her one more time. I knew that I would never see her again. For I am just a bed. And she is just as an empty glove.

Chapter Twenty-One

5-A

*A*fter Melinda died, my life changed. I spent the next few years, for the most part, in the empty house. I would watch the sunrise through a window on the east side of the house. As for the sunset, all I could see was the reflection of its red and yellow colors off of the wall on the opposite side of the room.

At first, on holidays or weekends in the summer months, many family members would come to the house and spend time together. They would sit and talk about old times and good memories. They would talk about how Grandpa Tom and Grandma Melinda taught and expected them to have self respect and confidence. Soon the confidence they had gained started to lead everybody in different directions. Pretty soon everyone was so busy that fewer and fewer people showed up. The weeks got longer and then they would turn into months.

Tom Jr. and Elaine were getting older and felt that if no one was going to use the old home place, that it would be best to sell it. It would be best if it was sold and settled before Tom Jr. or Elaine passed away. Within days of their decision to sell, there was a date set for an estate sale. Tom Jr. had come with a man from an auction company to sell off furniture and other items from around the house. Everything was catalogued and assigned a number. For the first time in 240 years I was known as more than the "tree", or the "bed." Now I was 5-A, the nightstand was 5-B, and the dresser was 5-C.

When I was a tree, there were billions more just like me. When I was a bed, there were millions of bed. But how many beds are known as 5-A? It was not my name, but it was something that identified me. It was to let people know that if they wanted me, they would have to give an item number instead of just "that old oak bed." It was like putting Mr. or Mrs. In front of someone's name. Or else like walking with a large group of people down the road where no one knows the others but someone calls you by your name. They were able to identify you and you reacted because you heard your name and you knew they were talking to you. Then you become more than just a person, you become an individual.

As the items to be sold were tagged and inventory was taken, the man with Tom Jr. shook his head and said that he would see him bright and early Saturday morning. After he left, Tom Jr. walked through every room in the house. He remembered little things that he had done and things that had happened in every room. As he walked into his parents' room, he sat down on me. He remembered stories his parents had told him of how he and his sister were born in that very bed. As he sat and remembered, I could feel an old, gray-haired man of 77 slip back into a five year old boy. He was running barefoot across the oak floor trying to get to the front door. He remembered that when his father got home from everyday from work, that if he was not at the door to greet him, then his day was not complete.

Tom Jr. wished that he could keep everything the way it was, or even bring it home with him. But he knew that he could not keep everything that he wanted, for his life was already full with his children and grandchildren. And the memories that he had would last him the rest of his life.

Saturday came and the house was opened by strangers. People that I had never seen before came piling in. They were looking at things like people in a shopping mall. It didn't matter if it was possessions that it took a lifetime to acquire. They just wanted a good deal on something that they could turn a quick profit on.

There was the china that Tom got for Melinda for their first anniversary that she had worked for nearly 70 years to keep chip free. There was silverware that Tom had spent over three weeks salary on and hoped that Melinda would never find out. There were trinkets and what-knots and old books that Tom and Melinda had read many times through the years. And then there was me. "5-A." Before, we were the things that dreams were built around. Now we sit as objects to the highest bidders.

It seems that through my long life there have been so many ups and downs. One of the highest points, it seems, has finally hit bottom. When you reach a low point that would not or could not get any worse, just hold on. If you have no control, then you can't change directions anyway. It is said that even in the desert, the wind sometimes changes directions, so there is still hope. When I was cut down and turned into lumber, it seemed bad. But after I got used to the idea of being a bed, I realized that I was just another object with a different lesson to learn. It seemed to all work out.

I was sold to the highest bidder. It wasn't long before I was taken apart and loaded onto the back of a truck. As I was taken outside for the first time since I was given as a gift to Tom and Melinda I looked to see if my stump was still there. Not only was it gone, but there was an old house sitting over the spot where I once stood. I looked around to see if there was anything familiar, and I saw nothing. Even the house that I was in was changed. As Tom's family grew, so did the number of rooms, which were added on. The outside changed from white paint to vinyl siding. And the roof from wooden shingles to composition.

There had been so many houses built that I could no longer see any natural beauty that I had seen in the past. And then the back of the truck was shut. It was something. I was delivered in a horse and wagon and I was removed in a truck. A span of time had passed and no one, except me, seemed to notice. I was delivered to a simple time to a simple place. And then, when I was moved it was different. Maybe not worse, just different.

My truck ride lasted about two hours. As it pulled up and parked, I was expecting the door to open, but it did not. I sat in that dark, cold, metal truck for a week. The only light that I saw was from the crack in the back door. It took me back to when I was an acorn, buried all winter. As I started to sprout, I would push up the soil and every day the crack got larger and soon I broke through. But this crack is the same every day. At the end of the week, the truck starts again, then rolls about a minute, then stops. The door opens and I am inside a large building. I am unloaded and put into a smaller room with other furniture that looks to be as old as I am.

Although the room is full of furniture, I am alone. Surrounded by empty shells of past dreams. At one time, they were trees also. Alive, with a history. Where were trees that these relics were made from grown? Who passed under them? Were they on a mountain or by an Indian village? When they were "harvested" and made into furniture, were they given as a special wedding gift like I was? Where these other beds as blessed as I? Did they experience the wonderful miracle of childbirth or the pain of death as they feel the soul leave the body of someone who died in them? Did they listen to quiet conversations that started as disagreements when a man and woman would lay down and discuss their day? Were they able to see them solve their disagreements then end it with a goodnight kiss? Did the cedar chest in the corner hold the dreams of a young girl as her parents moved west in a covered wagon?

These things are now important to man because of their age, or that someone famous owned them in the past. To me they are important because they were once lives. They were cut down by man because of a need for furniture.

We all become special for one reason or another to somebody or something. Some are more special than others and some become special for what they are worth. I have been special to others my whole life. From the best acorn for a squirrel, the best tree for a nest and lumber and the best wedding gift a father can give his son. The most special gift given to me was to myself. When I accepted who I was. I have not been able to move or accomplish tasks but I have been able to learn and remember. And that will be who I am until I am no longer. Whether I am a tree, a bed, or an object that just occupies a room full of old furniture.

Chapter Twenty-Two

Memories For Sale

As I sit in this room for months, each week someone comes in and gets a few pieces and brings them out . Sometimes the truck comes in and delivers more. The ones that are taken out are gone for a few days. When they return they have been refinished or repaired. Then, they are loaded on a truck and never seen again. When my turn came, I was taken into a room which resembled the shop where I was made into a bed.

I was reassembled and inspected. The nick in my headboard that was made when Tom Jr. knocked over a lamp while playing hide-and-seek with Elaine, was repaired. The slight scratches from a belt buckle that were made when Tom Sr. hung his trousers over the corner post were polished off. Every mark that was left behind to remind me of a specific incident in time was gone. The slate of my life wiped clean.

I was left as an old woman that would have just put on some make-up, trying to transform old knowledge into new innocence. I was no longer what I had become, but I was what someone else wanted me to be.

I was then placed into a truck and once again, I took a trip. This time I ended up in here, in this old antique furniture store.

I was assembled in my own little corner. Above my headboard is a painting of a window with real curtains hanging across it. It is a painting of a mountain sunrise. It is so realistic that I can almost feel myself slipping back nearly 80 years ago, when Melinda would open a window and a cool breeze would blow through the house and gently rustle the lace on a throw pillow that was left on the bedspread after it was made. I could feel the sun as it slowly rose above the mountains, giving birth to a new day. I could see other bed room suites laid out as if in a home. But they were not in homes. It is a store and we are just set in empty shells that do not make a home. It is just enough to spark imagination for someone to see what we could look like in a real room. I have seen many times in my life where man has tried to make himself look like something that he is not. It is always to show something to someone else. When he is alone he is content with who he is and what he has. When someone else is present he starts to paint a picture of someone who he wishes he could be. Even though the other person would accept him as he is or even help him if he needed him to. If man could focus the time and energy toward impressing himself first, then the others would automatically see a true reflection of the man he wishes to be.

After I am set in the right location there are pictures of people I have never known sitting on the dresser. An old lamp and windup clock were placed beside me on the nightstand. The room is set up to appear as if it was a memory captured from someone's past. It is a play on emotions and peoples desires to relive days that are gone. Though their life is filled with relics, past times will never be again. For even one second is worth as much as 50 years. If it has already passed then it is already history. It is gone and will never return.

The knowledge that I have gained in my life is truly from the past. My long life has left me with good memories as well as bad ones. I often recall scenes from my past of a more simple time. But instead of trying to travel into the past and hiding, I use it as lessons learned to control and build my future. I cannot control my physical outcome for I am just a bed moved around by man. But my dreams are all positive and my knowledge is built from my experience and it will continue to grow. If I never use it, it will not be a loss, for I have passed my time by learning. If, by some chance, I would need it and never have gained it, it would be to me and whoever else I could help, a loss that could never be regained.

Chapter Twenty-Three

Someone Sees Me

I have been in this shop for two years. There have been people who have come by and each one has had a different opinion. "Oh, that sure is a nice bedroom suite, but it sure ain't worth the price their asking for it." Or else, "The reason that it is so cheap is because it is a piece of junk." I have even heard, "That is a good price. If I had that much money, I would sure love to have it." But the one that I will always remember is when a man and his teenage daughter came in and was not really looking to buy anything. I was sitting, listening for the sound of the bell on the door. Each time it would ring the door would open and someone would walk in or out. Each time it rang was another chance for a new beginning. If someone would buy me, it would be a chance to become part of another family. But, as time passed so did hope, and I began to be content where I was. This particular time it rang they walked in as if they were in a museum. Just walking around, discussing how old the items appeared to be, and where they might have come from. As they walked by me, the man stopped and put his hand on one of my corner posts. He glanced at the dresser and then at the nightstand and then he stared at me. The look in his eyes looked as if he had seen an old friend. I've had people look at me before for what I was. This time was different. He seemed to be looking at me for who I was. He turned to his daughter and said, "Hey, Konni, look at this." As she turned and walked to her dad, he said, "Put your hand on this bed. Just look at it for a minute. If you look close, you can see that someone put a lot of time and effort into building it. You can tell by the wear that it was used a long time. It seems like it has a personality and a long history behind it, that began a long time before it was a bed."

"What do you mean?" asked his daughter.

"Well," he said, "People never think of things like before it was a bed, it was a tree and an acorn. It could have been over 100 years old before it was made into a bed. It could have overlooked an Indian village or had an outlaw hanged from its branches. It could have been in the woods by a school that your great grandfather attended in the 1800's where he sat and ate his lunch."

"Oh dad," Konni said, "sometimes you have a wild imagination."

"Well," said her dad, "a good imagination is a good thing. It is where dreams are conceived and reality is born. Imagination is the starting point of knowledge an success. And the best way to start is to take time to look at things just like this bed. Appreciate it for what it is, what it was and what it contributed to some family. It may be just a bed to most people, but to the people who first owned it, it was a special part of their life. It was important enough to keep so long and cared for so well. And if it could talk, it would probably be able to tell enough stories of love and disappointment to fill a book."

"Well, I guess you're right, dad. But the shop is about to close so we better go."

As they turned and walked toward the door, I wanted to scream and beg for them to stop. For someone almost felt who I was and understood me and showed me respect, even though I am just an object. As he laid his hand upon me, he was able to feel more than just a bed. And in return, I was able to feel more than just a man. Though his hand was calloused and showed the nearly 50 years or so that he has lived was spent working hard. Not only by his calloused hands, but by many scars that covered not only his body, but his heart as well. I could feel that each scar was a wound at one point and the deepest ones were on his heart. He had taken time to let time do its best work. To heal. I could feel that the things that left the scars to this man had become knowledge. I could feel no hate or remorse. For his time was too precious to lose, that time could be turned into something positive. It was evident in the time that he took to show his daughter that you cannot just walk by something. You have to take time to appreciate it. You must stop and take the time to look and touch it, and when you do your life, mind, and heart is opened up to a whole new world and centuries of history that so many people walk by and never get a chance to experience because they never have time to connect. As this man left, I could feel that there was still hope for mankind. He had taken the time to instill a seed of hope in his child and probably many others. And as I found many years ago from a little brown squirrel, if you plant a seed or an acorn something must grow. As we grow, the shape we take will determine what or who we truly become. So, if I must sit in this shop for eternity, I will at least have my knowledge and good memories to pass my time. For even with an eternity I now realize that time is too important to waste.

Chapter Twenty-Four

A Different Kind Of Ending

*N*ow, I hope that you have learned something from this story about an acorn, an oak tree, and a bed.

Our lives are similar to this story. But, unlike this bed, most of us can get up and move to accomplish goals in life. Even those who may be restricted by paralysis or the loss of limbs can lead productive lives filled with accomplishment as well as anyone else. It is only our minds that set limits on our bodies. With dreams and hope and a little bit of patience, we can learn and gain enough confidence to walk right through the door of limitations that we place upon ourselves. We can make contact with a whole new world that we thought only existed for others.

To some, much is given. But to most of us, we must work and earn what we have or what we accomplish and through that hard work, we learn to appreciate ourselves and others. For some it may take longer than others but if you don't quit and just hang in there, you are just as much a success as the winner.

My father used to tell me, "Son, I'd rather people see me die trying than quitting." It may take a year or it may take nearly 250 years, but the end will always be better than the beginning. Even the tree/bed had a purpose. Would you like to hear it ?

And when the bed had finished thinking about its past life, even though it was not able to move or interact, it found the importance of love, hope, and time.

It heard the bell on the shop door ring. He looked to see who had come in, since the shop was closed. But to his surprise, the door did not open or close. Just then the bed felt someone, and he could see the image of a man sitting upon him. He was dressed in a snow white robe. Around his waist was a beautiful purple scarf made of silk. Upon his feet were sandals that were made of leather, that no animal had died for. In his hand he held an hourglass. The bottom half was nearly full. In the top there were only a few grains of sand left. He sat quietly and still until the last grain had passed through to the bottom. When the top of the hourglass was empty, he stood up and ran the end of the scarf that was around his waist between the globe and a spindle on the hourglass and hung it by his side.

"It is time." He said, breaking the silence in the shop. As he stepped back, he stretched out his hand toward the bed and said, "arise, James."

Just then the old oak bed began to feel a sensation that it had never felt before. It felt as if the man's hand was pulling his soul out of the bed. Then he realized that he was actually moving of his own will.

"What is going on?" asked the bed. Then he realized that he had talked.

"Hello, James," said the man. "My name is Gabriel."

As he turned toward Gabriel he could see the

91

image of himself in the mirror that was on the dresser. The reflection that he saw was of an angel that stood over six feet tall. He was also dressed in white. Underneath the scarf that was around his waist was a large bag made with gold cloth. No longer was he a tree or a bed. He was an angel with a body that had arms and legs.

"What am I?" asked James.

"Well," said Gabriel. "You are a special angel. The large bag that is under your belt is filled with the knowledge that you have gained through your long life. You were sent here nearly 250 years ago to set in a forest so you could learn patience. Then you were set in a place where you could observe many people. How they were and how they have become over time. You have learned to love the people around you and to truly care for them even though you got nothing in return. Many would have been filled with hate or remorse for not being able to interact or communicate. But you used the time you were given very wisely. You have earned a special place in the hearts of so many."

James took the bag from his side and looked inside of it. He found knowledge and wisdom and so many things that he had learned throughout his life. Looking puzzled he closed the bag and placed it back underneath his belt.

Then he said to Gabriel, "There are many things in this bag. But of everything that I found, I did not find love at all."

"Oh, James. Love is a special thing, it could never be contained in a bag.

It must be nurtured in the heart. The only reason

everything else is in the bag is because your heart is so full."

As James smiled Gabriel placed his hand on his shoulder. "You know, Tom and Melinda have been waiting to see you for some time now."

As they turned to walk away, the little bell on the door rang twice, the door did not open or close, but the shop was empty, and so was the old oak bed.

8:46 PM March 20, 2007

Dedicated to the memory of my father,
James J. Wallace Sr.

*Thank you for teaching me not to see
what things are but what they can be.*

Samuel Hugh Wallace

CPSIA information can be obtained at www.ICGtesting.com
Printed in the USA
LVOW050302091112

306517LV00002BA/7/P